COFFEE AND CALICOS

THE MATCHMAKING BAKER

ROSIE PEASE

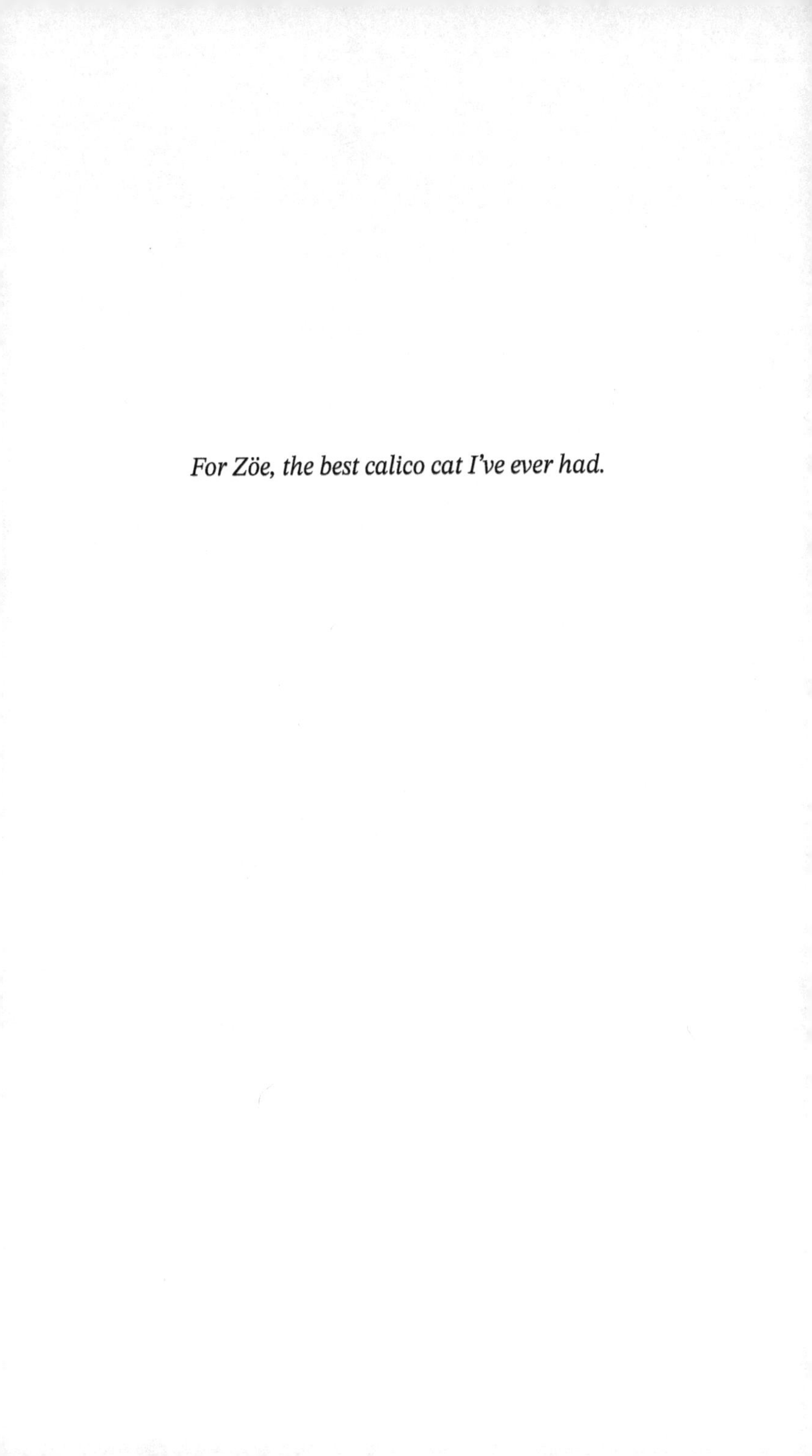

For Zöe, the best calico cat I've ever had.

About This Book

It better not be another ghost.

After moving to escape someone no one else could see, I finally got my own apartment. Ghosts have followed me around since childhood, but between unpacking and culinary classes, I don't have time to deal with wayward spirits.

Mom and Gram say they've warded my new place against ghosts, whatever that means, but soon, things begin to fall over, move around, and roll across the floor.

I may not be as alone as I had hoped. Will an uninvited roommate chase me out before I can settle in? Or will I be forced to live with the dead once again?

Author's Note

Dear Reader,

Thank you so much for picking *Coffee and Calicos* as your next read. If this is your first taste of my books, I hope you enjoy this short novella, which kicks off a whole universe of books. If you're finding this book after reading one of the Mixing Up Magic books, I hope you enjoy this earlier look into Joanie's life. Or maybe you're reading it after starting the Purrfect Travel Companion. You'll run into Meredith's familiar face in this story as well.

You see, this book, while primarily being about Joanie, features main characters in at least three series, possibly four if my muses cooperate, and alludes to at least one more. Fiddlefern Fjord, New England, where all of these books take place, is hopping with all sorts of mysteries, from the contemporary to the paranormal, and from the personal to the caper to murder. Stick around, you're sure to find something you like.

I love hearing from my readers. If you'd like to reach

out to me, you can find me throughout social media @WriteRosiePease.

Happy reading!

Cheers,

Rosie

CHAPTER 1

"Just don't do anything to burn the house down while I'm gone, okay?" I asked with my hand on the cut-glass doorknob of the front door to my apartment. "I'd like to get that deposit back next year when I move out." If I moved out. If I *really* liked the place, I'd stay until graduation, but that was a decision for another day.

"Yes, yes, dear. You know this is more smoke than fire, right?" Gram said as she waved her hand over a bundle of sage leaves, sending the smoke out into the corner of my beige-colored living room. Her beaded stone bracelets clinked together with each movement. She never took them off, said they kept her "energy aligned," whatever that meant. She'd been new-age since before that's what it was called.

"Joanie, you really should learn a bit more about this," my mom added. She waved the sage smoke out an open window that looked down on the two-lane road below and the house across the street. Two streets beyond that was the beginning of Baycliff Harbor, but I couldn't see it from the window.

"I think I've seen all I need to see to know what you're doing."

Mom closed the window and shivered, a common reaction when one stood by an open window in January, but it had helped to cut the acrid scent of the burning sage. "You don't even know what it's called."

"You're saging or whatever it's called, I don't know." I shrugged, my hand still on the knob. "To keep the bad spirits out." I knew they meant well, but I didn't care what they called it or what it did as long as it kept them happy and out of the boxes I still had to unpack. If they got their hands on them, I wouldn't be able to find anything until it was time to pack everything again.

I sighed. "Okay, well, don't set off a smoke alarm, please? I'll be home soon. I just need to go to campus and get some stuff."

After getting mere grunts from Mom and Gram in acknowledgment, I pulled open the door leading into the hallway. This was my first time ever living alone. For the past two and a half years, I had lived in college dorms, and before that it had been Mom and me in my childhood home. Now it was just me in my one-bedroom apartment, but there were five other units in my building. Most, if not all, of the other tenants were students at the nearby college.

"Hey, did either of you put a paper bag out here?" Sitting in front of me was a large plain brown paper bag, the kind people get when they order Chinese food or sandwiches. I had become very familiar with this type of bag during my time at school so far, but we hadn't ordered any food yet today. That was the plan for when I got back. It was well past lunchtime, and I was way too tired to cook after loading mom's station wagon last night, driving with her and Gram the four hours it took to get here from home, then unloading everything. Mom and Gram had helped me load the car—just as they had two weeks ago when they helped me move out of my dorm—but once we got to the apartment, they were done after the first trip up. I couldn't say I blamed them. They weren't used to all the stairs.

"No, dear, not me." Gram cast a quick glance over her shoulder to see what I'd been talking about before returning to her—

"Smudging! That's what you call it." The term had finally come to me.

"Very good, dear."

"Mom, did you?"

"Not me," she answered, not even bothering to look. She'd moved on to the open doorway between my living room and the kitchen. Mom was just as new-agey as Gram, if not more so, although Mom didn't wear bracelets like Gram did. She said they got in the way and instead wore rings and necklaces. Mom didn't understand how I wasn't more like the two of them. That sort of stuff wasn't my thing, although I'd helped Gram countless times with whatever it was she did. She called them rituals or even sometimes spells, but I think the spell part of it anyway was just to make it more fun for me and my cousin, who also helped sometimes. Beyond what she'd tell me to hold or where to stand, I'd never paid too much attention to what she'd done, but as a kid, I always thought the stones and feathers she used were pretty.

"Well, I'm going to set it inside right here," I said, pointing to a clear spot on the floor. "I'll deal with it when I get back, I guess." I picked it up. The weight shifted, but barely, and whatever it was inside wasn't that heavy. Maybe it was a housewarming present from one of my new neighbors, but what college student did that? Some strange prank was more like it. I gave the bag a quick sniff. At least whatever it was didn't smell.

"All right," they said in unison, dismissing me without looking.

Stepping out into the hallway that separated my apartment from my neighbor's, I closed the door behind me. I'd have locked it but figured I didn't need to with Mom and Gram inside. We never locked our doors back home, but I'd heard stories while living on campus that quickly broke me of that habit.

I walked to the central staircase that wound its way down to the first floor. I'd lose the notorious freshman—and an additional sophomore—fifteen in no time with having to walk up and down three flights of stairs every time I needed to go in or out of my apartment.

"Now, let's see how fast I can get to campus and back," I said to myself as I took my gloves out of the pockets of my peacoat and slid them on. I wanted to get back into the warmth of my apartment as fast as I could.

Behind me, a cat meowed.

"Oh, hello, kitty." I turned toward it and squatted, holding my hand out.

The black cat stared at my mitten.

I pulled my hand away and removed the mitten before offering it again. This time, the cat approached my hand, taking a quick sniff before using my fingers to scratch behind her neck. I wiggled them around to help him.

"Do you live here?" The lease allowed pets with an extra deposit.

He—or she—didn't respond and instead walked past me toward the door, then sat and looked up at the handle.

"You want to go out?" But it was so cold. And there was another matter to contend with. "I don't know if you're allowed to go outside."

He glanced up at me before resuming his staring match with the door handle.

"Go on, scootch." I was not going to be responsible for losing someone's cat. How had he gotten into the hallway anyway?

As if listening, the cat backed up a few feet.

"Such a smart kitty. Thank you." I pulled my glove back on and opened the door. "Maybe I'll see you later."

No sooner had I stepped onto the small porch than the cat was in front of me on the sidewalk.

"No way. I made sure you were still behind me." I would have seen it get past me. But it was the same cat, same few white hairs on its chest—it had to be. Just to be sure, I opened the door behind me and peeked inside. No more cat.

Now I had to get him back inside.

"I guess you're smart and fast," I told the cat as I turned back around, pulling my glove off in hopes he'd want another scratch behind the ears.

The cat was gone.

CHAPTER 2

Drats. How could the cat have gotten out of my line of site so quickly? All I'd done was turn around, but now, I didn't see him anywhere.

I couldn't just leave now. The last thing I wanted to do was lose a neighbor's pet on my first day at the apartment. What a way to make an impression that would be.

"If I were a cat..." I mumbled, looking around. To the side of the porch was a large bush. Despite the winter weather, it was still green. I headed over to it. Maybe the cat had gotten scared and taken cover under its branches.

I stooped down, coming face to face with the underbrush, then had to get even lower onto my hands and knees. Thank goodness the ground was dry.

No cat.

"Here kitty, kitty. Where are you?" I repeated as I looked under the hedge going from the front of the house to the back.

Still nothing.

The rear of the house had been paved over for tenant parking, but I continued calling, adding in several *pspspsps* for good measure in hopes the cat would come to the noise.

After a few more minutes, I had to face facts. That cat wasn't going to come to me even if he could see me making a fool of myself out here.

"Joanie? What are you doing? I thought you'd left," Gram said as she poked her head out the open window.

"I tried," I said with a shrug and drawing my lips to the side. "But then I let out a neighbor's cat, and I can't find him anywhere."

Gram smiled slightly, a comforting look of concern. "You get going to campus. I'll take a break up here and see if I can coax the cat back inside. You know I have a way with them."

That was an understatement. She and her cat Sterling seemed to have conversations with one another. One-sided, of course. He didn't talk, of course, he was a cat after all, but somehow, he always knew what she wanted him to do.

"Are you sure?"

"Positive. You go on and get back so we can have lunch."

There was no arguing with her, and besides, I didn't want to be out in the cold any longer than I had to anymore. If anyone was going to find the cat, it would be Gram.

I nodded but couldn't help scanning the area once more for the black cat. "Thanks. I'll be back soon!"

Campus had been advertised as being a ten-minute walk away from my apartment, which described itself on the flyer I saw as being in a "prime location for student housing." We'd see about that. Today was a good test because I only needed to pick up the materials that were required for my Savory Bakes 304 class, which was starting in a few days. I was studying sweet pastries for my major in baking and pastry arts, but it wouldn't hurt to learn more about the savory side of things too. I liked having a wide foundation of knowledge. I never knew when I might need it. And what if I ever had to—or chose to—branch out?

January Term, the name given to three of the five weeks between semesters and referred to as J-Term throughout the college, was probably the best time for me to take the extra class. My schedule during the rest of the school year was already crowded with my attempt to take business prerequisites for my eventual master's degree. I planned to get one after I graduated with my bachelor's in a year and a half. I needed it. Someday, I'd open my own bakery in some small town. I'd grown up in one. Its winter population was 1,208 and grew to just over 2,100 in the summer. After living in a Baycliff now for a few years, I knew cities weren't for me. They were too big, too crowded, and too anonymous. I liked the idea of knowing everyone and being able to walk everywhere I needed to go to. There was just something about the small-town vibe that made even a day like today—

freezing with a blowing wind—that much more bearable.

As I scurried down the sidewalk toward campus, doubt crept into my thoughts. I couldn't believe I had moved in between semesters. As if I didn't have enough to do with January Term starting in a few days. Either one—moving or the class—alone I could handle, but between the unpacking, the intense study, and the requisite baking for three weeks to pass the class, I wasn't sure if I would manage. How was I supposed to practice my recipes for class? My kitchen wasn't even set up properly. I was glad to finally have my own, though, so that was something, at least. Plus, moving was a better option than the alternative of staying in my dorm for a few reasons, and once my kitchen was ready, there'd be nothing stopping me from working my kitchen magic.

It wasn't real magic, of course, although several of my friends said that's how good my cooking and baking was. Gram regularly called me a kitchen witch too.

Magic.

If only.

Now that would be a unique way to market a bakery.

I laughed out loud at the absurdity of my thoughts, and the cold air nearly took my breath away. I pulled my hood tighter around my head and quickened my pace. Campus was just around the corner.

And if the black furry tail disappearing around the stone pillar marking the campus entrance was any indication, so was the cat.

CHAPTER 3

I hurried after the cat, arriving on campus right at what felt like ten minutes. It probably would have taken me fifteen at a normal gait, but between the wind off the water making it feel even colder and spotting the cat from a couple blocks away, I'd picked up my pace.

From the campus entrance—no sign of the cat—there was a short paved path cutting across the quad to the bookstore and the promise of coffee at the student-run café next to it. No way was I going to go back home without warming up some first.

Campus was almost eerily quiet. I shouldn't have expected anything less since it was between semesters. I was surprised anyone was around at all, but I knew there had to be others like me who would soon be taking a J-Term. They likely hadn't all returned after going home for the holidays. After all, most didn't have to move before classes started.

The door to the central building automatically slid open as I swiped my student ID card at the security box.

I rushed inside, grateful for the burst of hot air from the vent directly overhead. If it wasn't for the threat of the door opening again and letting a gust of cold wind through the glass vestibule, I would have just stood there basking in the warmth.

"Hey," the clerk behind the checkout counter greeted me as I entered the bookstore, giving me a polite nod before brushing his shaggy blond hair out of his eyes with both of his hands.

"How are you?" I asked with a smile as I breezed in and headed to the premade supply kits in the back corner. The special baking kit had been put together by my professor, a chef who specialized in savory pastries. Chef Patterson had been the executive chef at the restaurant he'd founded, Patterson's, for years before stepping down and entrusting his prodigy with his legacy. I promised myself it was where I'd like to go to celebrate graduating with my master's in two and a half years from now. Distance wasn't an issue, it was only a short bus ride away into the city center, but it might take me that long to afford it. Now Chef Patterson taught Savory Bakes 304 and a couple of other classes in the major, which gave him more time to spend with his family. Word across campus was he'd recently had a second grandchild and that she already had him wrapped around her finger.

I looked at the premade kit and gasped at the price tag. College was not cheap. Although I didn't need a ton of books, now that I'd finished my general education requirements, I couldn't escape a semester without a heavy credit card charge from the bookstore. The kit would double several of the supplies I already had, but this was more convenient and ensured I had everything. Paying for this kit was a better option than tearing through my still-boxed kitchen goods and checking items off the supply list as I found them. That would have been too much to deal with. I already hated the idea of having to unpack everything, and it's not even like I had a lot of stuff. All of it could fit into my mom's car, aside from the furniture I'd bought before break and had delivered shortly after we got to the apartment. Thank goodness we hadn't hit traffic. What a pain it would have been to reschedule the delivery if I hadn't been able to meet the truck. Most of what I had was kitchen or food related. Besides, it wasn't like everything I was getting in this kit wouldn't come in handy eventually. This was what I was going to school for. Baking would be my career. If I didn't need it at home someday, the bakery I dreamed of opening likely would. It was an investment, or at least that's what I told myself to feel better.

I took the kit up to the guy at the counter. He was wearing a baggy sweatshirt and jeans, which would have broken protocol had he done so during the semester.

He noticed me looking and offered an explanation. "I asked first. Since there aren't classes yet, I don't have to be in my uniform." His answer sounded rehearsed, making it seem like he'd given the same statement several times today.

During the semester, everyone had to wear their checkered pants and a white chef jacket, with a colored collar attached to tell everyone what majors we were taking. Green for baking and pastry, blue for culinary arts, yellow for nutrition. Teacher's aides wore red. We even had to wear our chef hats unless it was windy or raining.

I blushed and placed my kit on the counter between us. "I wondered. What are you taking?"

"Culinary arts." He smiled and brushed his hair out of his eyes again, but it immediately fell back into place. I bet he did that often. It would have driven me crazy if my hair were like that. As it was, I almost always had my brown hair tied back into a ponytail. He likely had to wear a hair net or gel it in addition to having his chef hat on when classes were in session. "What about you?"

"Pastry."

"You like it?" He rung up my kit, whistling at the price.

"Sure do." I chuckled and handed him my credit card. "I'm going to open my own bakery someday. You?"

"Barbeque food truck." He swiped my card through the register, then passed it back to me.

"Oh, fun." Those had gotten huge in Baycliff during my two and a half years here. That was one of the positives of living in the city—the variety of food. Food trucks were no exception. There were even french fry and grilled cheese trucks. They frequented campus on a regular rotation. Many of the owners were graduates from the school. "I don't think I've seen one of those yet around here."

He placed my kit in a bag and set it on the counter for me to grab. "If all goes as planned, I should be the first barbeque truck in Baycliff this summer."

"Good luck," I told him as I took my kit and turned away from the counter.

"You too."

I gave him a quick wave over my shoulder as I exited the bookstore and made a beeline for the coffee shop, checking to see if I could spot the cat with every step. No luck.

I'd never been much of a coffee drinker before college, preferring tea instead, but I had definitely changed my ways once I got here. Coffee fueled me, keeping me upright on some days, giving me a chance to socialize now and then, and warming me up like it was about to do today. The freshly ground coffee bean aroma smacked me in the face as I stepped inside, rejuvenating me a little just from the scent. I was grateful for it being open. The barista, who was in her chef uniform with a red apron emblazoned with the coffee shop logo over it, was equally happy to see me.

"Joanie!" Meredith waved. "How goes the move?"

"It goes. I'm going to have to get used to walking up all those stairs, though. Definitely going to miss living on the first floor in the dorm." That was probably the only thing I'd miss, minus the few friends, like Meredith, I'd made in my wing. "Quiet day?"

"It's been dead in here. I don't know why they insisted we be open during break." She sighed. "Probably because this is a franchise."

Despite it being a college-owned franchise, it was completely student run, but they still had rules to follow. When I first saw how much the coffee was cutting into my budget, I had at one point contemplated getting a job here and had read all about it.

I nodded in agreement and looked up at the menu board.

"Jess was here earlier, but she only had a half shift. So jealous." I could feel her studying me as I thought about what I wanted. It didn't make deciding any easier.

"Do you still have the eggnog mocha or was that only a December thing?"

She pivoted and looked at the pump bottles of different flavors behind her. "Let me check if we still have the syrup in the back. It was wicked popular." She, like me, was born and raised in New England. Words like *wicked* were in our DNA.

Meredith darted through a swinging door behind the counter and reappeared moments later with a container full of translucent-beige liquid. "Last one. I just need to attach a pump, and one eggnog mocha will be coming right up. What size?"

"Grande, please."

"You got it." She unscrewed the cap and twisted on a pump. "So, I know I've asked this already, but tell me for real. How goes the move? I'm going to miss you on the floor, but I totally understand the allure of getting your own place."

Meredith had lived across the hall from me in our dorm. I couldn't tell her the real reason I had moved. I'd learned that lesson. Meredith thought I'd only moved so I could be on my own and have my own kitchen—that I was that serious about my studies. I was, but I'd made do with the communal kitchens for two and a half years. I could have survived if not for the other issues.

As she made my coffee, brewing a fresh pot to keep me talking longer, I filled her in on the layout of my new apartment—a central kitchen separating the living room from the bedroom. She laughed at my predicament of having so many stairs to climb but agreed it was a good way to get in shape. Being on the first floor of the dorm had made getting places so much easier, but that didn't outweigh the biggest issue it had.

"Here you go." Meredith handed me my eggnog mocha with whipped cream on top.

I bit the peak of the cream and smiled. "Thanks." I handed her my student ID card that was preloaded with dining money able to be used at any of the campus eateries. We had amazing food here, unsurprising for a college known for its culinary arts program.

I sat down with my mocha at one of the nearby tables, close to the window so I could watch for the cat. There was no sense in taking it outside with me. It would have cooled down too much by the time I made it back to the apartment, and Mom and Gram would only wonder where theirs were, even though neither one of them drank coffee. Upon their insistence, I had already unpacked my tea kettle and various loose teas for them in case they were in the mood to have anything while I was gone.

My mocha was still much too hot to drink, so once I was sure the cat wasn't in sight, I took out my syllabus for Savory Bakes 304 to see what we'd be focusing on.

Beyond seeing I had the premade kit to pick up, I hadn't given it much of a glance. I'd been too busy.

I flipped through the bulky syllabus. Chef Patterson had included all the recipes we'd be learning in class. Units focused on onions, various cheeses, meats, and spices. The recipes were making my stomach growl: caramelized onion and feta rolls, Cornish hand pies, braided pesto bread, and more. I'd have to get lunch soon and hoped Mom and Gram would be ready to eat once I got back to the apartment. I wasn't going to be able to wait long.

At the end of each unit, we had to create our own savory baked good for the class to sample. I already knew what I'd be making for the spice unit. *Lussekatter*, Swedish saffron buns that were traditionally made for St. Lucia Day. I'd learned the recipe when I was in junior high from my best friend's grandmother.

Scratch that.

Former best friend.

I was hit with a twinge of pain at the thought of my long-ago friend. We hadn't spoken in almost seven years even though we'd attended school together until gradua-tion, which wasn't even three years ago. Ginny and I had been best friends since kindergarten when I accidentally got sand in her face after flicking my shovel up in the sandbox after it got stuck on something. She laughed it off through a few tears. After I hugged her to apologize, we'd been inseparable.

That was until the day I confided in her that I could see ghosts when we were thirteen.

CHAPTER 4

I'd been able to see ghosts for much of my life, but in the beginning, I didn't know that's what they were. They looked just like living people. Not see-through, not glowing in any way, not hovering over the ground. They didn't walk through walls or tables out of habit, although I'd learned they could if they had to. When I was little, I thought Mom and I lived with more people than we actually did. But, no, it was just the two of us. At first she believed I had an overactive imagination, that these people were imaginary friends. That changed when I told her that a man who was a dead-ringer for her father regularly sat with us at dinner. She called Gram immediately after that confession.

As it turned out, I wasn't the first one in the family who could see ghosts. Gram's sister, Peggy, had been able to as well. It wasn't something that got talked about, so Mom had no idea that numerous imaginary friends was a sign I had that ability. It had turned Peggy into a recluse, needing to live alone so she wouldn't be surrounded by so many spirits. She even broke off all contact with Gram and the rest of the family, and she faded into obscurity, never brought up again until Mom called Gram about my issue. Mom hadn't even known she had an aunt until Gram told her during that conversation.

Gram told Mom to watch me and that as long as I was okay with what was happening, there was no need to intervene.

It took a couple years, but I learned who was a ghost and who was a real person based on how they interacted with the world. Ghosts, for obvious reasons, weren't social with the living even if they tagged along with a live person. The exception was small children. Ghosts liked to play with kids because the kids hadn't stopped being able to see them. It was like some curtain hadn't dropped yet, closing them off from the world beyond what most adults knew as normal. Almost everyone was born with the ability, but the capability ended after a few years as real life became more concrete for us.

For me, the curtain never closed. For years, I easily managed my ability. It was fun to have extra people in my life.

But as soon as I hit puberty, all of that changed. The regular ghosts remained, but new ones appeared. Ones that wanted my help. Ones that scared me. I don't know where they had been for the first twelve years of my life, but I wanted them to go back to wherever they had been. I tried helping the ghosts that needed it if I could. Some-times they needed me to listen. Those were easy—mostly. When they weren't, it was because what they had to say wasn't what anyone should have to hear. Those ones didn't necessarily scare me, though. The ones that did were bad news all around. I've since locked those memories away.

I tried to manage it on my own. I didn't even tell Mom at first because I had no memory of her ever talking to Gram about it. She'd taken her instructions literally. She watched me. For the most part, we'd never talked about the ghosts who visited us regularly ever again while I was a kid. She certainly didn't encourage my skill. As new-age as Mom has always been, I think this was over the top, even for her. Maybe it would have been more normal had Great Aunt Peggy stayed.

It went on for a year before things got to be too much. I had to confide in someone. Mom wasn't my first choice, though.

Ginny had been my best friend for over half my life. She seemed like she'd be a safe person to tell. Best friends forever, right?

At first she thought I was joking. Then I described her Grandma perfectly. The one I'd never met—not the one who showed me how to make the saffron buns—because she lived out in California and Ginny only visited her at Christmas and for two weeks in the summer until she died when we were ten. Ginny grew concerned with that until she said I could have seen a photo. She laughed at me, even when I protested and said it wasn't funny. That I wasn't joking. She said I could cut the act. So I described the periwinkle dress and ivory shoes her grandmother was buried in. For some reason, those were the clothes she had chosen to stay in for her ghostly form. Ghosts didn't change outfits but weren't locked into anything either. That had been another reason I could tell who they were. Ghosts wore the same thing day in and day out.

Talking about her grandmother's clothes did it for Ginny. She believed me, but she didn't accept it. She told me I was crazy and said she didn't want to hang out with me anymore.

I thought she'd be fine after the weekend. We'd had little tiffs before, but we'd always made up. On Monday, she didn't sit with me on the bus. She moved seats in all of the classes we had together. She sat at a different table at lunch. The cool kids adopted her, and she became one of them. From then on, she ignored me. I don't think she ever told anyone what happened, I never heard those rumors spreading in the halls, but she never talked to me again.

"You have not taken one sip of your eggnog mocha in the last five minutes." Meredith plopped into the seat in front of me. "Did I not make it okay?"

I shook all thoughts of Ginny from my head and looked at Meredith. "Sorry, what?"

"I asked if you liked your drink."

"Oh, yeah. I'm sure it's fine. Waiting for it to cool off and liking how it's keeping my hands warm. I ate the whipped cream before it melted."

"Ah, gotta keep those taste buds working properly, right?" She winked at me.

"You got it." The last thing I needed while in a culinary program was to burn my tongue on hot coffee and screw up my ability to taste for the day. I needed to be able to taste my food as well as those of my professors and classmates. How else was I supposed to grasp subtleties of each dish's flavor?

"I understand completely. So where'd you zone off to? I like to pretend I'm on a tropical island. Especially in this weather." She waved her hand at the window in a displaying fashion.

"Oh, I didn't go anywhere that time. I was just thinking."

"Must be some deep thoughts. You gave yourself a crease right"—she pointed to in between her eyebrows—"here." She laughed. "I wouldn't go doing that too often."

I joined her in her laughter. They did say it was the best medicine. "I'll try not to."

I lifted the cap of my mocha and blew into the cup, then drew a small sip to confirm the temperature was safe.

"Good, right?" she asked.

"Mmm . . . It's perfect." I took another, longer, sip. "This is one drink I wouldn't mind having all year."

"You never did become much of an iced coffee person, even in the summer."

I glanced out the window for the cat once more while answering, "Nope." She'd tried to introduce me to the concept of having ice-cold coffee when we moved into our dorm freshman year since I'd never had it, but after giving it try—several times at her insistence that they didn't make it right, and once more after she got the job here and she could do it the "right way"—she'd left me to my hot coffee year round. Just like I left her to her iced coffee even in the dead of winter. I wasn't surprised to see one on the table in front of her.

"Won't you get in trouble for not being behind the counter?" I asked.

"Who's here to tell on me?" She made a show of looking around the room, even standing up and spinning in a circle. We were the only two people in the coffee shop. "I'm not going to say anything if you aren't."

I made a motion of zipping my lips closed.

"See? I knew I liked you." She laughed again as she sat back into the chair.

We chatted and drank coffee for the next half hour or so until someone else came into the shop. She darted up from the chair and hurried behind the counter to take his order. I glanced over at the exchange. It was the guy from the bookstore. He'd put a gray beanie on, covering his blond hair, but the sweatshirt was the same shade of navy.

I took that as my cue to leave. I needed to get back to my apartment. Hopefully it was still standing. I bet Mom and Gram would be done with their smudging by now. It wasn't a big apartment. I caught Meredith's eye as I headed for the door and gave her a quick wave before exiting the coffee shop.

CHAPTER 5

The wind had died down by the time I started my trek home. It helped the temperature some. Now it was just cold instead of freezing.

Still no sign of the cat.

I walked my usual pace down the sidewalk leading away from campus, passing a gas station, a laundromat I'd likely be frequenting since my apartment didn't have a washing machine or dryer, and two pizza places. I'd passed a few ghosts too, but they were all carrying on with their normal afterlives and didn't pay me much attention. Two years into my abilities, I'd learned if I didn't let them know I saw them, they had no idea I could. Gram had seen to that when I finally confided in Mom about my spirit troubles.

Gram wasn't an expert or anything, but I guess she had learned a thing or two from dealing with her sister, and somehow—with her crystals, feathers, and some awful-tasting tea she had me drink—she locked that portion of my ability away or blocked me from being contacted by bad spirits. I'd asked her to make it all go away, but she'd said that would have changed me too much.

Maybe I'd understand that reasoning someday.

A ghost was why I'd moved into my apartment. Of course I'd end up in the one dorm on campus that had spirit activity. Despite all of the rumors that surrounded colleges, a majority of schools didn't have real hauntings. Most ghosts didn't want to stay at school for their entire afterlives. This one wasn't done with his partying ways, however, and it was driving me crazy. Somehow, he'd figured out what I could do, so he flocked to me like those little striped brown birds that stole dropped french fries at the outdoor patios on campus. He constantly wanted me to party with him. He'd show up to my room drunk, stand right outside the doorway, and beg me to hang out with him. If the door was closed, he'd pound on it. Unsurprisingly no one else could hear it, so it wasn't like I had backup in complaining about a noisy neighbor. Just a pillow to cover my ears when I was trying to sleep. Thank goodness he actually couldn't get into my room, supposedly since Mom and Gram did the stuff with the sage and whatever else they did there too. I don't know what I would have done had he been able to get inside.

At first, I'd complained to the Department of Residential Life, saying I wanted to move buildings due to roommate issues—I didn't even have a roommate, but it was worth a shot—that I didn't like the first floor and the noise coming in from outside my window, anything sane I could think of. I certainly couldn't tell them the real reason. Unfortunately, the school didn't have any open rooms in another dorm, so I began looking at the ads, hoping I'd find something off campus. It took a few months, but I finally found something that would work for me. Mom and Gram didn't need some elaborate explanations as to why I wanted to move. They jumped on board my plan as soon as I said *ghost*. I loved them for that.

I glanced down at my watch as I climbed the four concrete steps to the door of my building. "Fifteen minutes." Exactly like I'd thought.

As I lifted my hand to open the front door, the knob turned. The door swung open to reveal a petite brunette wearing a sky-blue parka. She jumped back as she looked up at me with a gaze that matched her coat.

"Oh! Sorry," she gasped. "I didn't see you there."

"Apologies are mine for startling you."

Seemingly recovered from the surprise of my standing there, she turned on a bright smile and stuck out a gloved hand. "I'm Belle. You must be the new tenant."

"Joanie, nice to meet you."

"Likewise." She looked down at the kit in my hand. "Culinary student?"

I nodded. "You?"

She shook her head. "Library studies. Over at the state school. Housing was a bit cheaper this far out, even with your school up the street, and the buses are free for us students, so I jumped on saving a few bucks."

"Makes sense. Thanks for the reminder about the

bus." Campus had its own shuttle for store trips, so I'd forgotten about the student perk.

"Well, it was nice to meet you, but speaking about buses, if I don't go, I'm going to miss mine."

"Oh, sure, sure. Nice to meet you too." I stepped out of the way, so Belle could pass.

She smiled at me once more. "Have a good one."

I watched her go down the steps before thinking to ask, "Hey, earlier there was a black cat. It got outside. I didn't mean to—"

Belle turned to face me but continued walking backward to the curb. "Ah, that's all right. Must have been Bandit. He can go outside."

"Is he yours?"

"Nope. Don't know whose he is, exactly. Maybe everyone's. They call him a neighborhood cat. You'll see him all over the place."

"Thanks. That makes me feel better." I let out a sigh of relief. At least I hadn't let him escape. "Guess I'll see you around."

"Bye," she said cheerfully before turning and jogging up the sidewalk. I hoped she'd make the bus.

As I stepped inside, closing the door behind me, I let out a hard sigh as I looked up the first flight of stairs. This was going to take some getting used to. I'd be better off in the end. It had been way too easy to put on the freshman fifteen when I moved here. Two years later, I still hadn't lost it all.

I took off my coat before even reaching my door. Three flights of climbing had made me uncomfortably warm. I'd need to get a coat tree or some sort of a hook to put by the door if I was always going to have it off before walking in. I'd add it to the list of things I still needed to buy. Mom and Gram had already started one for me.

I dug my keys out of my purse and unlocked my apartment door. It stuck a little bit, but I pushed it open with a bit of extra oomph. I stepped in and pulled the door closed behind me.

All was not right with my apartment.

CHAPTER 6

I called out to them, worried that something had happened. "Mom? Gram?"

"Oh good, you're back," my mom said as she breezed into the living room. "We were starting to wonder if you'd gotten lost. Let's order food from somewhere. I think I saw a pizza place not too far away when we drove here."

"Are you two okay?"

"Yes, dear," Gram answered as she followed a few feet behind my mom. "Why wouldn't we be?" She still had a sage bundle in her hand. Had they been doing that the entire time I'd been gone? Just how much smudging did my apartment need?

The remote for the TV had been knocked off the coffee table in front of the couch. They were the only two pieces of furniture set up in the room, thanks to the furniture delivery people who'd put them together earlier. My water bottle was on the floor, no longer on the stool I was using as an end table.

"Look at this place. It's a mess." How could they not see everything I did?

My mom stifled a giggle. "Of course it's a mess. You just moved in. Your stuff is supposed to be everywhere."

"You seriously don't see it?" I didn't know how she could have missed it all.

The more I looked, the more I saw. The only reason my lamp hadn't hit the floor was because its cord was too short. It leaned against the arm of the couch, the cord pulled taut. "Did you bump the stool and not realize you nearly broke my lamp in the process?"

Mom shrugged. "I mean, I guess that could have happened. But there's no need to get so worked up about it."

On the floor to the side of the room sat a plastic bag full of stuff from one of my dresser drawers back home. It looked like it had been rifled through. It was open and one of the handles had been pulled down. A few of the smaller things that had once been inside it had rolled several inches away.

"Really, dear, I think you're feeling a bit over-whelmed," Gram added. "Especially after that black cat got out. Afraid to say I didn't find him."

"That's okay. One of the neighbors said he's a neigh-borhood cat."

Gram nodded understandingly. "Then I guess you'll be seeing him again soon enough."

I surveyed the small space some more. A tube of lip balm, which had been in the plastic bag, was across the room. I guessed one of them could have kicked it without realizing, but why were they in that bag in the first place?

I pointed to the sage in Gram's hand.

"Are you sure the smudging worked? This apartment better not be haunted. My lease is for a year." I didn't know what stock I put in smudging, it seemed a little too witchy for me, but since they believed, I wanted their word that they had done their job.

Gram put her hands on my shoulders. "We smudged everything. More than once, even, just to be sure. We don't want anything to bother you while you're here. Did something happen?" She searched my gaze. "No, you seem fine outside of this."

"Is your blood sugar low?" Mom asked.

"You know I've never had a problem with that."

"When was the last time you ate? You don't have to have a problem with it for it to affect you sometimes."

"Breakfast. At the rest stop. But then I had a coffee at the shop next to the bookstore on campus. Too cold not to."

Gram snapped her fingers. "That would do it. Mel, will you—"

"Say no more," my mom interrupted. "I'll put the kettle on."

Gram placed her hand back on my shoulder. "You need to balance out all that caffeine. It's making you jittery in more ways than one. Your aura is all over the place."

"Gram, you know I don't believe in that stuff." Now I'd done it.

She put her hands on her hips. "You'd better start.

You'd have a better handle on yourself if you opened yourself up to it." She sighed. "You can see ghosts. Why won't you believe me when I say I can see colors around people?"

"I can only handle one weird thing, and you've got to admit, ghosts are a pretty big thing."

"You let us do the smudging, though. That's not what you'd consider normal."

"That's true, I don't, but I figure it can't hurt."

Gram shook her head as she tried to hide an eye roll.

"Plus, it keeps you two busy and out of my stuff. Or it did until now." I pointed at the open plastic bag.

"I swear we haven't touched your things."

"But—"

She turned and walked toward it, pointing. "It probably fell over on its own. We've all been hurrying around to get you situated in here."

I nodded. "Maybe you're right." By the time I was almost done with unpacking Mom's car, I no longer cared where I was throwing things. I'd just wanted it out of my hands so I could get the next load.

"Tea's steeping!" Mom called from the kitchen.

"There, now," Gram said soothingly. "Why don't you go grab your mug, then we can sit down and figure out what we're eating."

"Okay, let me hang up my coat." I walked back over to the door and hung the coat on the knob. "I was thinking we could go out and grab a coat um—"

That's when I saw it.

The paper bag I had put inside the door from the

hallway was tipped over and open. Had I unknowingly invited a ghost inside in my rush to leave?

"Um, what?" Gram asked.

I turned around to face her, but my gaze kept falling to the bag on the floor, distracting me from my thought as I answered. "Um, a coat-umbrella thingie, you know one of those stands." I extended my arm above me to show Gram the height of the thing I couldn't remember the name of. I snapped my fingers as it came back to me, "A coat tree," but my eyes remained focused on the bag.

"What are you looking at?"

"Did either of you open the paper bag I put here before I left?"

Mom walked back into the room at that moment, taking a sip out of a purple mug. "Bag?" She had no idea what I was talking about.

I pointed to it at my feet.

"Honestly, I forgot all about it."

"What was in it?" Gram asked.

"That's the thing. I never looked." I stooped and picked it up. It was a noticeably lighter. "It wasn't heavy, but whatever was in it is gone now." I placed it back on the ground and stood.

"Are you sure there was something in it?"

That earned my mom a look. "I'm pretty sure I would have figured out if it was empty the first time I picked it up." I placed my hands on my hips and realized I got this stance from both her and Gram now that I could see I mirrored their poses almost exactly.

Mom held up her arms in surrender. "Sorry. I still think you're overwhelmed with everything going on."

She took a seat on the far side of the couch and set her mug down on the coffee table. "Yours is on the counter. I poured one for you too, Mom."

Gram walked back over to me and linked her arm through mine. "Come. Let's get that tea." She led me into the yellow and blue kitchen, half-pulling.

"Gram, you can't just bring a ghost inside without knowing, can you? What if that's what was in that bag?"

She dropped my arm when we made it to the stove. She grabbed her tea, then handed me my purple mug. I blew on the surface of the steaming liquid. It had become second-nature to me. Almost instinctual.

"Without knowing? I don't think so," she answered, then took a small sip of her tea. "That's part of why we put wards on your doors after we smudged."

"Wards?" More witchy stuff I didn't quite believe in.

Gram rolled her eyes. "You really should learn about your heritage."

"How will I learn if you don't tell me?" I batted my eyelashes at her.

She tried to stifle a grin and failed. "Wards keep ghosts outside. But if you invite one in, they can cross your threshold. Don't know why you'd do it willingly, but I'm really not sure if you can do it without knowing it." She clapped her hand on my shoulder. "Just don't bring any antiques into the apartment and you should be fine."

"But what about—"

"That bag? Do you think a ghost would attach itself to something so disposable? No, the object has to mean something."

"Could it have been in the bag?"

"Well, I guess anything is possible, but maybe whatever it was rolled away like the things in that plastic bag." She spun me around and gave me a small shove toward the living room. "Come on, I'm hungry. Let's look at those takeout menus."

I sat on the couch, opposite my mom. Gram smushed in the middle. I pulled the blanket that I was half-sitting on out from under me.

"*Riaoww!*"

CHAPTER 7

I shot up to my feet as quick as lightning.

"What was that!"

Gram stood up, too, grabbing the blanket I had been in the process of moving. She pushed back one of the folded portions. "I think we've found your ghost."

"What?"

She stepped back, revealing a small calico kitten. She wasn't a baby, but she was far from full-grown. A few months old, then.

My mom gasped. "A kitten!"

It took off like a shot and skittered around one of my boxes, jostling a few things in another bag as it scurried away to hide.

I followed the kitten quietly and lifted the box it had run behind, then placed the box on top of another one at my side. I squatted down and shifted another box away from where I thought the kitten had gone after that.

"There you are," I cooed, hoping a soft voice would calm it down.

It hissed. It was one of the cutest noises I'd ever heard.

"Oh, come now," I said in not quite a whisper. "It's all right. I'm not going to hurt you." I stuck my hand close to the kitten so it could smell me and realize I was okay.

Instead, it batted at my finger.

"Oof, you've got some sharps claws there, don't ya?" I kept my fingers still and avoided eye-contact. I didn't want to scare her any more than she already was. At least I assumed it was a she and not one of those one-in-three-thousand calico males.

She whacked away at my hand for several moments until I finally felt a little nose press against my knuckle.

"There we go, see? I'm not scary." I slowly wiggled my finger back and forth.

When the kitten didn't bat at it, I inched my hand closer to her until I could pet the top of her head with one finger. She didn't react, which I took as a positive sign. At least she hadn't shrunk back. I added another finger, then another, before sliding my hand down to scratch under her neck.

That seemed to do the trick. The little calico melted into my touch.

At that point, I knew I had her. I reached in with my other hand and scooped her up.

She froze as I brought her to my chest and stood up, but with some more neck scratching, she relaxed into my hold. I studied her. She had a white belly with patches of ginger-tabby and black on her back and head. Her little pink nose had a tiny black line running down the center of it.

"She's so cute," Gram squealed quietly.

"But where did she come from?" Mom asked.

I ticked my head back and to the side to indicate the paper bag tipped over by the door. "She's probably what was in that."

"Aww, the poor thing." Mom got up from the couch and walked over to the paper bag on the floor. "Who would do such a thing?" She picked up the bag and peeked inside. "There's a note."

I hadn't looked inside the bag when I picked it back up. It hadn't felt like there was anything left in it.

Gram didn't miss a beat. "Well, what does it say?" she asked as Mom reached inside and unfolded the piece of paper. She let the bag fall to the floor.

Mom turned the paper and read aloud, "My cat had kittens a while back, and I have been trying to find homes for them. I can't take care of them all. You look like a good person. Please give this girl a good home. She's cute but a bit sassy. Thank you. All the best." She dropped her hand with the note to her side. "It's not signed."

"Well, that explains that, then," Gram said.

"Explains what?" I asked as I continued staring at the kitten sitting contentedly in my arms as I pet her.

"How everything you claim got moved, moved." Gram pointed to the things that had rolled out of the plastic bag. "That little one woke up, freaked, got out of the bag, and ran around before hiding under the blanket on the couch."

I nodded. It certainly made sense.

"Joanie," my mom began. "What are you going to do

with it?"

"What do you mean what am I going to do with it?"

"Surely, you aren't keeping it."

"Of course I'm keeping her." It wasn't a hard decision. Someone had dropped her off on my doorstep. I certainly wasn't going to be the second person to abandon her, even if the first had good intentions. She was meant for me.

"You just moved in. You go to school full time. You have a work-study job."

"She's a cat. It's not like I need to take her for walks multiple times a day or worry about her eating my couch cushions." The kitten had started to purr. "Besides, she likes me."

"Oh, come now, Mel." With those four words, I knew Gram was on my side. She always was. "You know as well as I do that familiars just come to you. They find a way. *This* is the way." What in the world was a familiar?

I could tell Mom was getting worked up. I didn't really think she was upset about me getting a cat. She was probably more hangry than anything. I got the same way. She pointed at me with an open hand. "But she's a poor college student."

She wasn't wrong about that, but how expensive could having a kitten be? After the initial vet visits, of course. I hadn't forgotten about those.

"It will work itself out." Gram winked at me as Mom huffed and returned to the couch. Gram slid over to where I had been sitting to give her some room. "So what are you going to name her?"

"Um . . ." I looked down at the kitten, who now

appeared to be sleeping. "Sassy? That's what the note said she was."

The kitten cracked one eye open and glared at me.

"Okay, not Sassy. Dolly?"

She continued her one-eyed stare.

"Does she look like a Dolly?" Gram asked.

I shrugged. "No, not really."

Gram scratched her chin, her thinking stance. "Well, something will come to you."

I nodded, and the calico started to squirm. She was ready to get down.

"But in the meantime, can we figure out what we're eating?" Mom asked.

"Sure. Then we need to go out and get some stuff for the kitten." I put her on the floor, and she darted toward the tube of lip balm I had yet to pick up. She smacked it, and it spun across the floor. She pounced on it, then smacked it again.

"And let's not forget your coat tree," Gram said.

I walked back toward the coffee table and picked up a menu. "Pizza?"

They both nodded.

"About time," Mom added.

We ordered a large Hawaiian pizza with pepperoni instead of ham and several sides. We never could make up our minds when it came to what we wanted to eat, so we typically ordered way more than we needed. But that meant I would have leftovers for a few days.

After we ate, we ran to several stores, including a furniture shop. Gram was adamant that I get my coat tree if that's what I wanted. She got that way sometimes, and I had learned to run with it. I also had no groceries, so we had to fix that. With the addition of the kitten, I needed to get a litter box, cat food, dishes for her food and water, and a couple of toys. She couldn't play with my lip balm forever. As I searched for the right coat tree while Mom was off looking at hallway mirrors, Gram walked over to me with two silver candlesticks and an envelope, a devious grin on her face.

"Shh . . . For the kitten." She passed me the envelope. Opening it, I saw several twenty-dollar bills inside.

"Gram, you don't have to do this."

She winked and said, "Don't tell your mother."

It would be our secret. "Thank you." I gave her a big hug.

"And I'm getting these for you too." She held up the candlesticks. "You never know when they might be useful." I wasn't going to argue. They were pretty, and living in an area with ice storms, occasionally heavy snowfall, and the odd hurricane, I figured if the power ever went out, they would come in handy. What else would I need candlesticks for?

Gram and Mom left for a nearby hotel shortly after we got back to the apartment. It allowed me to set up things for the kitten and to unpack my bedroom a bit so I could at least sleep in there tonight instead of on the couch. They came back and took me out for dinner before they returned to their room for the night. We'd go out for breakfast in the morning before they got on the road.

That night, the kitten curled up with me on my bed, right between my knees.

CHAPTER 8

J-Term was flying by. Week two was almost over already. I'd been enjoying learning all about making savory breads and hand pies. My favorite so far had been the caramelized onion and feta bread. The rosemary lemon rolls had come in at a close second. With all of the food I'd been getting to bring home after class, in addition to practicing at home, I hadn't gotten takeout once. My wallet was better off for it. Besides, I needed that money for cat stuff now.

Part of J-Term's intensity was that it had morning and afternoon sessions with only an hour in between the two. I typically went home to have at least a half hour to eat lunch and play with the kitten, but it was gently snowing today, and I didn't want to walk through it until I had to at the end of the day. If it was still snowing, of course. The weather here was such that it could change within minutes. Instead, I hung out in the campus coffee shop during my free hour.

They'd finally run out of eggnog mocha after the first

three days of J-Term. Apparently, I wasn't the only one who liked it. I switched to drinking peppermint lattes after Meredith promised they would be available until spring. I was a creature of habit and liked sticking to one drink.

Meredith plopped into the seat across from me and set her iced coffee on the table. She was on a break between her J-Term sessions too. "I am exhausted. Remind me not to do a J-Term next year. I'm going to want one last vacation before having to enter the real world after graduation."

I smiled and blew on my drink. Still too hot. "Will do. But didn't I tell you to do that this year?"

"Yeah, but I really mean it for next year." She laughed. "And I still need to work a half shift when class ends. I don't know what I was thinking."

"That you wanted to try something different and couldn't add it into your semester schedule. Or was that just me?"

"Nope, that pretty much sums it up." She took a long sip of her iced coffee, then stirred her straw through it, the ice cubes softly clunking against one another.

"Hey, do you remember that guy who works in the bookstore?"

Her already round eyes grew wide. "Yeah, why wouldn't I? He comes in to the coffee shop practically every day."

I was glad she'd noticed him in here as much as I had. It affirmed the feelings I had whenever I saw them in the same vicinity. They were hard to describe, a cross between a tingling in my toes to butterflies in my stomach. The sensation told me one thing, though. Meredith and Dan were supposed to be together.

"Why?" she asked. "Are you interested in him?"

"Me?" I pointed at myself. "Ha! No."

She visibly relaxed.

"But the next time he comes in when you're working, you should get his number," I suggested.

She dismissed my statement with a wave. "I've sworn off men."

I knew that was nonsense. "Uh-huh, sure." I blew on my latte once more and waited for her to bite.

She leaned closer and propped her arms up on the table with her elbows. "Why? Do you think he's interested?" She rested her chin in her hands and asked, "Did he say something to you?"

I could have laughed at how quickly she changed her tune about guys when she thought one was into her. "I just have a really good feeling about the two of you is all."

"You sure?"

I nodded. "I've never been wrong."

And I hadn't been. Not that I regularly tried to pair people up—that was more my mom's forte. But I had been good in high school at setting up my friends with dates to dances or whatever other events were going on. If the two save the date announcements hanging on my fridge were any indication, my matches stuck, especially the ones where I got tingly toes and butterflies in my stomach when I saw them together before making the pairing.

Meredith sighed then grabbed her iced coffee and drew a long sip through her straw. "He *is* cute."

"Mm-hmm," I said in fake agreement, not that she'd be able to tell I thought otherwise. He wasn't my type. I didn't like the shaggy hair look, and he was much too laid back for me, if my brief interactions with him had told me anything, but Meredith didn't need to know that.

"You know? I'm going to do it. I'm going to get his number."

"Good for you. Let me know how it goes." I blew across the surface of my coffee for a final time and chanced a sip.

Perfect.

That evening, once I was finally home from my second class, I decided to experiment with the lussekatter. After feeding the kitten and having a leftover Cornish hand pie for dinner, I cleaned up and got ready.

Our next to last unit was on saffron. It was a yellow to red spice that gave foods a golden hue that came from a particular variety of crocus that had a short growing season and had to be picked by hand. The flavor was a little hard to describe. I wasn't sure any two people could taste the same thing when they had it. For me it was a slightly sweet honey-like flavor. Mom didn't like it at all, as we discovered the first time I made lussekatter as a teen. She said it was bitter.

This was the unit I had been planning for since before term started. I laid out all of my ingredients, setting out my *mis en place* just like I'd learned years ago when I took my first kids' cooking class at the community center in my town.

"Now where's the saffron?" I knew I had it. Not only did I have a small tin from the supply kit to use in class, I had gotten a slightly larger tube of it to practice with at home. It wasn't cheap. I had paid over twenty dollars for three grams of the spice. But after putting everything else I'd need on my counter, I couldn't find either container anywhere.

The kitten came trotting into the kitchen and sat down at my feet.

"Hi, kitty."

She looked up at me and meowed, a short little chirp I believed meant hello. She used it whenever she walked into a room I was in.

This calico had proven to have a ton of personality, even in just the two short weeks I'd had her. She shook her tail when she got excited, which happened every time I fed her. Sometimes she got so riled up as she ate, and she'd half-growled, half-meowed as she chowed down. It was the funniest thing. She'd taken to curling up on the back of the couch when I wasn't home. I often found her there as I walked into the apartment until her head shot up when she realized I was there, and then she'd scamper into the kitchen to be fed. That cat loved her food.

But whenever I curled up on the couch to read, she'd hop down from her perch and claim the spot either at the end of my feet where my blanket bunched up or on my legs. At night, she always slept right in between my knees. I was still getting used to the cramps I'd wake up with because I never wanted to disturb her by moving when she was on me. Fortunately, the cramps always went away after a few minutes of walking around.

She'd gotten a clean bill of health from the vet when she went for her first round of shots, and she'd get fixed in the few days I had between the end of J-Term and the start of the next semester.

Everything was working out.

Except I still hadn't figured out a name for her.

She meowed at me again.

"Have you seen my saffron? You know my spices aren't toys. I told you that when you took the marjoram I needed to infuse with the cream cheese." We were working on her not jumping up on the counter. She was getting better about it, but she wasn't perfect. Then again, who was?

She stood up and immediately sat back down and meowed.

"That doesn't tell me anything." I put my hands on my hips. "Did you take the saffron?"

Once again, she stood up and sat back down, spinning in a tight circle before sitting for good measure.

"Saffron. Have you seen it?"

She stood up once more, looked me dead in the eye, and sat back down.

"Saff-ron," I said slowly, drawing out each syllable. Why was I talking with my cat like she'd know what I was saying if I said it slower than normal? At this rate, I saw a lifetime of being the crazy cat lady ahead of me.

She meowed. Slowly, drawing out both the *me* and the *ow* for a few seconds. Just like I'd done with her.

"Are you mimicking me?" I crossed my arms and stared at her.

She was clearly unimpressed. If cats had eyebrows like humans did, I'd swear she raised one at me in response.

"If you're not careful, it's going to be your name," I threatened. I had stooped to a new level. I wasn't going to *be* a crazy cat lady—I already was one.

She stood up on her hind legs and reached up my leg.

"Saffron? Really?"

She tapped me with one paw twice in quick succession as if patting me for a job well done.

"All right, then. Saffron it is."

She sat back down.

"But I'm calling you Saffy for short."

She got up and walked out of the room, dismissing me with a flick of her tail.

Mere moments later, the larger container of saffron rolled into the kitchen from the living room, stopping only when it hit my foot. The tiny threads of spice were no worse for the wear.

If I hadn't known any better, I would have thought she planned it.

At that moment, I peered out the window to see Bandit on the fire escape. I'd see him there occasionally, as well as in the hallway and on my walks to and from class. Sometimes even through the windows of other apartment buildings. A true neighborhood cat like Belle had said.

As if realizing I was watching, he turned to me and winked, practically smiling as he did.

But cats couldn't do that.

It was just a coincidence. Or a play of the light. Something.

Right?

Matchmaking, baking, and ghosts… a recipe for disaster or a spell for success?

Joanie's magical story is just beginning. Join her as she follows her baking dreams in *Cookies and Curses*,

Book One of the Mixing Up Magic series, available now.

WHAT'S NEXT?

Matchmaking, baking, and ghosts... a recipe for disaster or a spell for success?

I've never been wrong with cookies or love, and it's made my bakery popular in my small town. Rumors claim my matchmaking skills come from a dash of magic in my treats, but I can ignore the gossip about me being a witch.

But ghosts only I can see suddenly needing my help? That was never a part of my business plan, and solving their problems might be more than I can handle.

If I can't figure out the mystery of why they're coming between the couples I've connected, then not only will my matches not get their happily ever afters but failing could conjure the end of my livelihood too. I can't let the cookie crumble on my career.

Ghosts, it's time to meet your baker.

Cookies and Curses **is now available.**
Grab it today to continue reading Joanie's magical story.

About the Author

Rosie Pease is a native Rhode Islander but has lived in Vermont, New York, and Ohio. She uses the places she's traveled to as inspiration for the settings of her cozy mysteries, pulling the theater from one, the cider mill from another, the river from another to create a fictitious town that feels familiar.

She collects Funko Pops of the Harry Potter, Hunger Games, Doctor Who, DC TV, and Marvel variety, with a few others thrown in for fun. Her desk is a mess, but she can find everything on it, so it works for her as long as things aren't falling onto the keyboard as she writes.

When she's not crafting cozy mysteries, she's playing with her daughter, hanging out with her husband, or being amused by her two crazy cats.

Come find Rosie online:
Website: https://rosiepease.com
Facebook, Instagram, Twitter, and Pinterest:
@WriteRosiePease

ALSO BY ROSIE PEASE

The Matchmaking Baker

Coffee and Calicos

Sweets and Santa

Mixing Up Magic

Cookies and Curses

Scones and Spells

Weddings and Witchcraft

Potluck and Powers

Muffins and Mediums

Purrfect Travel Companion

Catastrophe on the Road

Catastrophe in the Kitchen

SAMUEL
FLEMING

TALES
FROM
ANOTHER
WORLD
VOLUME 4

ii

Copyright © 2022 by Samuel Fleming

Cover Design by MiblArt

ISBN-13: 978-1-954679-46-7 (paperback)
ISBN-13: 978-1-954679-45-0 (ebook)